How to Rescue a Gorilla:

1. Gain their trust by
   complimenting them.

I LIKE YOUR FACE!

2. Try to
   persude them
   down by waggling a tempting
   banana *or two* at them.

3. Suggest they leap to safety
   onto the handy trampoline you keep
   under your hat.

MR BOUNCE TRAMPOLINE

4. If all else fails,
   phone the fire
   brigade and/or a
   helpful grown-up
   (if you know any).

Ω

PEACHTREE PUBLISHERS
1700 Chattahoochee Avenue
Atlanta, Georgia 30318-2112
www.peachtree-online.com

Text and illustrations © 2015 by Alex T. Smith

First published in the United Kingdom in 2015 by Hodder Children's Books
First United States version published in 2017 by Peachtree Publishers

Artwork created digitally. Title is hand lettered;
text is typeset in Italian Garamond BT.

Printed and bound in May 2017 in China by RR Donnelley & Sons

10 9 8 7 6 5 4 3 2 1
First Edition

DEC 0 6 2017

ISBN 978-1-68263-009-9

Cataloging-in-Publication Data is available from the Library of Congress.

CLAUDE

On the Big Screen

ALEX T. SMITH

PEACHTREE
ATLANTA

Chapter 1

In a house on Waggy Avenue,
number 112 to be exact,
there lives a dog named Claude.

4

Claude is a dog.
Claude is a small dog.
Claude is a small, plump dog
who wears the snazziest of
sweaters and a jaunty red beret.

jaunty red beret

snazzy sweater

Claude lives with his best friend Sir Bobblysock, who is both a sock and quite bobbly.

He also lives with Mr. and Mrs. Shinyshoes.

Every day Claude waits for them
to shout "Cheerio!" and skip out
of the door to work, then he and
Sir Bobblysock have an adventure.

Where will our two chums go
today?

Chapter 2

One morning (it was a Thursday) Claude was in the garden with his beret on, and he was being VERY busy and important.

Sir Bobblysock was out there too, lying on a sun chair with his cardigan around his shoulders.

It was the first time he'd been out
of the house for a week, as he'd
had a chill all down one side.

Claude was busily and importantly
hanging out all his costumes to dry.

"There!" he said, stepping back to admire his handiwork. "Now it is time for a treat!"

Claude whipped his beret off and had a jolly good rummage around until he found what he was looking for—a gigantic box with a trampoline inside.

It had arrived in the mail the other
day—a present from one of
Claude's friends who had a circus.

Claude set up the trampoline and started to bounce.

Up and down Claude went, high up in the air. His ears flapped about beautifully behind him.

"Come and have a go!" Claude called to Sir Bobblysock.

Sir Bobblysock said that he'd love to, but he'd just had a pastry and didn't want it coming back up again with all the bobbling about.

Claude continued to bounce. The higher he got, the more he could see of Waggy Avenue.

There was Miss Highkick-Spin jazz-stepping her way to the dance studio.

14

And there was
Mr. Lovelybuns
sprucing up his
buns.

15

And there was a giant
gorilla in a dressing gown,
drinking a cup of tea.

A GORILLA??

IN A DRESSING
GOWN??

DRINKING
A CUP OF TEA??

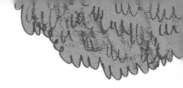

What on earth was a giant
gorilla doing on Waggy Avenue?

Claude's eyebrows started to
waggle. His bottom started to
wobble, and his tail began to
wag so fast it was a blur.

Quickly, Claude stopped
bouncing and stashed the
trampoline back in his beret.

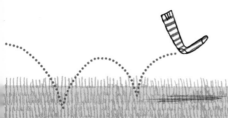

"I am going to investigate this gorilla!" he cried, and ran off with Sir Bobblysock bouncing along behind him.

Unfortunately, in his excitement to find out what was going on, Claude managed to get his foot caught in a dangly bit of the clothesline and— TWAAAANNNNGGGGG!— the whole thing fell down.

"Oh bother!" he said and quickly stuffed all his costumes back in his beret without even taking them off the line.

Then Claude and Sir Bobblysock went through the front door, down the steps, and out onto Waggy Avenue.

Chapter 3

Oh my! Was there ever such a lot to take in! Claude had never seen Waggy Avenue quite like this before.

Everywhere he and Sir Bobblysock
looked there were gigantic spotlights,
whirring cameras, and big fluffy
microphones poking out.

Claude was just ogling at it
all, when he tripped over a bit
of clothesline that had
escaped from his beret. Three
somersaults later, he landed
SMACK BANG in front of one
of the film cameras!

He was just thinking what a splendid landing that was—bent knees, no wobble, GORGEOUS smile—when someone shouted "CUT!" and marched over to Claude. The man looked very frowny despite the fact that he was also wearing a nice hat, which was currently at the jauntiest of angles.

"What are you doing!?" cried the man. "Can't you see that we are in the middle of making a film? You just tumbled into our shot!"

Claude quickly stuffed the dangly bit of clothesline back under his beret, smoothed his sweater down over his tummy, and said "sorry" in his nicest voice. This seemed to make the man with the megaphone much happier.

"It's OK," he said. "It was only a rehearsal. My name is Everard Zoom-Lens, and I am directing this film called *Gorilla Thriller!* It stars these two actors here—Errol Heart-Throb and Gloria Swoon."

Claude introduced himself and Sir
Bobblysock. Claude told Gloria
Swoon that he liked her dangly
earrings. Sir Bobblysock went a bit
pink when Errol Heart-Throb shook
his hand and felt ever so glad he'd
put his curlers in the night before.

"And this is our wonderful gorilla,"
said Everard. "His name is Alan."

The enormous gorilla
stood up and gave
Claude and Sir
Bobblysock a very
dramatic bow.

He'd been classically
trained.

"Would you like to watch us make our film?" asked Gloria.

Claude had never seen a film being made before so said, "Yes please!" in his Outdoor Voice. Sir Bobblysock had seen one before, years ago, but that's a different story.

"You can sit yourself down there and watch," said Everard Zoom-Lens. "There's lots for us to do before we can start filming properly."

So Claude and Sir Bobblysock
settled themselves down and
watched closely as Errol Heart-
Throb, Gloria Swoon, and the
gorilla rehearsed
their scene.

33

Chapter 4

From what Claude could gather, the film was about a giant gorilla who had escaped from the jungle and was now hoofing up the side of a building while waggling Gloria Swoon about in one of his gigantic hands. Errol had to rescue her by being very handsome and brave.

It was terribly exciting.

"Right!" said Everard eventually. "Everyone take five!"

Everyone shuffled off to their trailers to prepare for the afternoon's filming, leaving Claude and Sir Bobblysock alone.

First, Claude sat on his seat
and slurped a juice carton.
Sir Bobblysock nibbled a fig roll.

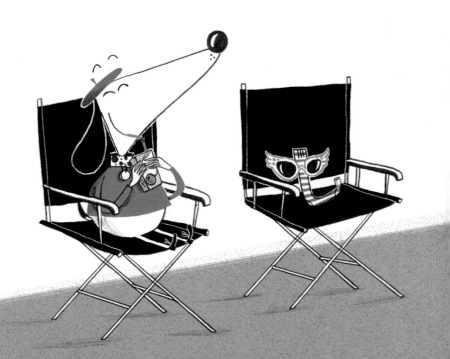

Then Claude swung his legs
for a bit and sighed.

Sitting down and waiting was
awfully boring sometimes.

Soon, Claude's eyes started
to wander...

Then his hands
wandered...

...and finally his legs followed.

He was just sneaking back to his
seat after some terrific snooping
when a bit of the clothesline
escaped from under his hat again.

"This is going to cause a terrible accident," he said. Claude tried to stuff it back under his beret, but it managed to wrap itself around one of his feet and...

41

Yowzer!

This time, Claude's landing wasn't anywhere near as splendid.

42

But at least his bottom
found somewhere soft to plop...

...on a

big

box of wigs!

FILM: GORILLA
THRILLER!

.WIGS.

Wigs, Claude discovered, were hairstyles that weren't attached to heads, which meant that you could try as many on as you wanted.

Claude thought he looked lovely with a full head of soft waves.

Sir Bobblysock decided to keep it all very casual.

Chapter 5

There you are!" said Everard
Zoom-Lens. "And you've
found the wigs! Good! Would you
be so kind as to help get them on
the actors so we can start filming?"

The two pals helped the actors put on their wigs. They did it VERY busily and VERY importantly.

FILM: GORILLA THRILLER!

.WIGS.

Errol Heart-Throb had one with a curlicue. He also had quite a ravishing fake mustache.

Gloria Swoon wore a blonde wig full of bouncy curls.

Alan had a terrifically stylish
toupee.

The next thing that needed to be done was make-up.

"We need them to look beautiful and very glamorous!" said Everard through his megaphone.

Claude thought faces weren't THAT different from coloring books. He also had some felt-tip pens, an emergency glue stick, and glitter in his beret.

As Everard dashed off to tell someone where they could put their bananas, Claude set to work.

The effect was rather striking.

"Erm-lovely," said Everard, not quite as excitedly as Claude had hoped. "Let's get into costumes and get this film started."

The actors and Alan bustled off to their trailers to get changed.

55

When they emerged again, they
looked like different people.

Claude clapped his paws together
and Sir Bobblysock
went a bit giddy at the
sight of Gloria's sequins.

"Places, please!" cried
Everard, and everyone
hurried into position.
He handed Claude and Sir
Bobblysock a list of jobs
that needed to be done
during the shoot.

57

Chapter 6

The first thing was to hold a long microphone on a very long stick. It was ever so heavy and made Claude wobble this way and that.

He came VERY close to whacking
a big piece of set. Luckily, Sir
Bobblysock was on hand and a
disaster was averted.

But all this meant that Claude
and Sir Bobblysock were too busy
to notice the clothesline start to
snake its way out from
Claude's beret again...

The next job was to
swish a large spotlight
about so that it
followed Alan as
he swung down
Waggy Avenue.

Well, that was easier said than done. The light was so heavy, Claude had to get Sir Bobblysock to help, which he did.

Everard gave them a thumbs up.

Sir Bobblysock suddenly panicked. He thought he'd lost one of his contact lenses on the ground in all the excitement. Claude swung the light around so everyone could look for it. Then Sir Bobblysock remembered that he didn't actually wear contact lenses—he'd just read about someone who did in one of his magazines and got confused.

All this kerfuffle meant that no
one noticed as a bit more
of the clothesline
slipped out
and started to
drag across
the floor...

Soon it was time for the big final
scene to be recorded—the bit
where Alan had to swipe Gloria
Swoon away from Errol Heart-
Throb, just as he was giving her a
big sloppy kiss, and then shimmy
up the side of Miss Melons's shop.

Claude and Sir Bobblysock dashed
back to their seats so they could
get a good view of the action.

But, in all the rush, Claude didn't
see the clothesline with all his
costumes on it slip out from his
beret completely.

Claude also didn't see it get tangled
around some lights and cameras, or
around Gloria Swoon and Errol
Heart-Throb's feet.

Nor did he see it get knotted
around Everard Zoom-
Lens and his
megaphone...

Just as Errol Heart-Throb leaned in to kiss Gloria Swoon and Alan the gorilla dragged her up the building, the clothesline pulled tight and…

THUD!
CRAS
JANG

Miss Melons

Lights and
cameras tumbled
everywhere! Everard
fell on his bottom,
and Gloria Swoon and
Errol Heart-Throb went
flying across the street!

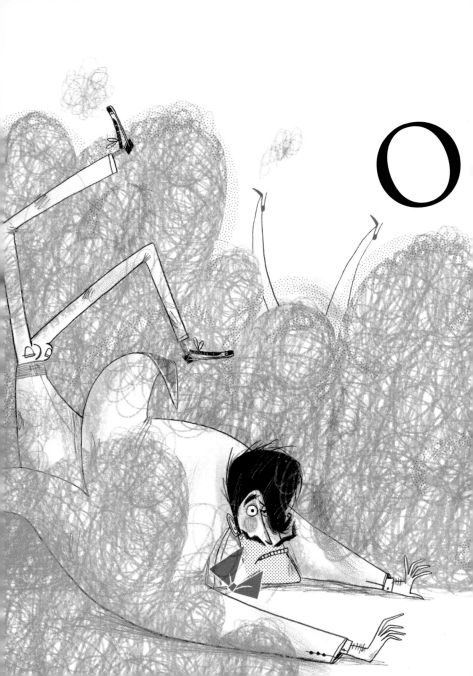

OOF!

"Uh oh..." said Claude.

Sir Bobblysock had one of his hot flashes and had to whip out his fan.

73

Chapter 7

When the dust settled, it became clear that all wasn't well.

Gloria and Errol had both twisted their ankles and had to go straight to the hospital.

As everyone dashed about to fix the mess, Everard Zoom-Lens let out a wail through his crumpled megaphone.

"Whatever will we do now?" he said. "We can't make a film with our two lead actors in the hospital! It's a disaster! If only we had two look-alikes who could stand in for them."

He slumped down in a chair and went ever so limp.

Claude looked at his feet and fiddled with the hem of his sweater. He'd accidentally caused this disaster with his clothesline full of costumes, and now he wanted to fix it. But what could he do?

Then he had an EXCELLENT idea!

"Sir Bobblysock and I could do it!"

Everard smiled sadly. "But you
don't look a bit like Errol or
Gloria."

Claude smiled a hearty grin
and reached into his beret.

"Just you wait!" he said.

The result was
MARVELOUS!

"Goodness me!" cried Everard Zoom-Lens. "You look JUST like Errol and Gloria—no one will ever know the difference! Extraordinary! Quick—let's get the cameras rolling! ACTION!"

What an afternoon Claude and Sir Bobblysock had!

OH NO! I WILL SAVE YOU!

Claude shouted
his lines in his best
Outdoor Voice
and he ran about
and lunged dramatically.

Sir Bobblysock turned out to be terribly good at fluttering his eyelashes, especially when Alan the Gorilla was giving him the willies.

Miss Melons'

LOVELY PEAR
Fruit and Vegetable
Emporium

And when Claude
bravely rescued Sir
Bobblysock and carried
him safely down the ladder
to the ground, everyone
clapped and hooted.

After Everard had shouted
"CUT!" he trotted over to
Claude and Sir Bobblysock,
grinning from ear-to-ear.

"You were STUPENDOUS!"
he said. "Truly wonderful!
Won't you come with us
to Hollywood and be
famous movie stars?"

But before Claude
could answer, there
came an enormous
sob from somewhere
above their heads.

Chapter 8

It was Alan.

He was standing on top of the roof, crying and fussing with his bow tie.

"What's the matter?"
cried Everard.

"I can't get down," said Alan between sobs.

"Use the ladder!"
said Everard.

But Alan wouldn't.

If there was one thing he was more frightened of than heights, it was climbing down a ladder.

"Oh no!" said Miss Melons. "I can't have my customers choosing their cabbages and picking their plums with a gigantic gorilla crying all over them!"

She was right, of course, but Claude wondered if he could help.

Was there some way of getting Alan down that was fun and not frightening?

Of course there was!

"Come on, Alan!" cried Claude from his trampoline. "This is a lot of fun!"

He carried on bouncing while Alan nervously shuffled closer to the edge.

Claude smiled his nice smile and even wagged his tail encouragingly.

At last, Alan covered his eyes,
took a deep breath and...

Miss Melons'

BOING!

"A movie star AND a gorilla rescuer!" beamed Everard, joining Claude and Alan for a bounce. "Are you sure you won't come and be a world famous actor?"

BOING!

Claude thought about it. He certainly liked dressing up and acting, but he also liked puttering about at home. And after the wigs, the sequins, and being manhandled by a giant gorilla, Sir Bobblysock desperately needed one of his nice long lie downs.

Claude explained all of this to Everard Zoom-Lens. He was disappointed, but understood.

"But you MUST keep all of the wigs!" he said, thrusting the box into Claude's paws. "You both did look SO fetching in them."

Claude and Sir Bobblysock thanked Everard Zoom-Lens, waved goodbye to all their new friends, and went home.

Chapter 9

Later that evening, when Mr. and Mrs. Shinyshoes returned home from work, they were jolly surprised not only to find a gorilla asleep in their kitchen, but to see that both he and Claude were wearing wigs.

"Do you think Claude knows anything about all this?" asked Mrs. Shinyshoes.

"Don't be silly!" said Mr. Shinyshoes. "Our Claude has been fast asleep all day."

But Claude DID know
something about it.

And we do too,
don't we?

Keep your eyes open for Claude and Sir Bobblysock.
You never know where they'll turn up next.

CLAUDE
at the Beach

A seaside holiday turns out to be more than Claude bargained for when he saves a swimmer, encounters pirates, and discovers treasure! HC: $12.95 / 978-1-56145-703-8, PB: $7.95 / 978-1-56145-919-3

CLAUDE
at the Circus

An ordinary walk in the park leads to a walk on a tightrope when Claude accidentally joins the circus and becomes the star of the show! HC: $12.95 / 978-1-56145-702-1, PB: $7.95 / 978-1-56145-980-3

CLAUDE
in the City

A visit to the city is delightful but ordinary until Claude accidentally foils a robbery and heals a whole waiting room full of patients! HC: $12.95 / 978-1-56145-697-0, PB: $7.95 / 978-1-56145-843-1

CLAUDE
in the Country

When a fearsome bull interrupts Claude's afternoon down on the farm, he must think like a cowboy to save the day! HC: $12.95 / 978-1-56145-918-6

CLAUDE
in the Spotlight

Claude is ready for his stage debut—but when a spooky theater ghost tries to ruin the performance, Claude knows the show must go on! HC: $12.95 / 978-1-56145-895-0

CLAUDE
on the Slopes

Claude loves the Snowy Mountains—but when his winter wonderland threatens to avalanche, he must make a daring rescue! HC: $12.95 / 978-1-56145-805-9, PB: $7.95 / 978-1-56145-923-0